WITHDRAWN
LVC BISHOP LIBRARY

LEBANON VALLEY COLLEGE LIBRARY

P9-DNO-006

THE DREA

a min**edition** book

published by Penguin Young Readers Group

Text and illustrations copyright © 2006 by Robert Ingpen

Coproduction with Michael Neugebauer Publishing Ltd., Hong Kong.

Rights arranged with "minedition" Rights and Licensing AG, Zurich, Switzerland.

All rights reserved. This book, or parts thereof, may not be reproduced in any form without permission in writing from the publisher, Penguin Young Readers Group, 345 Hudson Street,
New York, NY 10014.

The scanning, uploading and distribution of this book via the Internet or via any other means without the permission of the publisher is illegal and punishable by law. Please purchase only authorized electronic editions, and do not participate in or encourage electronic piracy of copyrighted materials. Your support of the author's rights is appreciated.

Published simultaneously in Canada.

Manufactured in Hong Kong by Wide World Ltd.

Typesetting in Alexa, headlines in Neugebauer Kursiv Zierbuchstaben

Color separation by Fotoreproduzioni Grafiche, Verona, Italy.

Library of Congress Cataloging-in-Publication Data available upon request.

ISBN 0-698-40036-4

10 9 8 7 6 5 4 3 2 1

First Impression

For more information please visit our website: www.minedition.com

MKEEPER

A letter to
Alice Elisabeth
from her grandfather,
Robert Ingpen

minedition

LEBANON VALLEY COLLEGE LIBRARY

Dear Alice –

This is a story about a man who collects dreams and keeps them safe. He is called The Dreamkeeper.

Nobody I know has ever seen him. We can only imagine what he looks like, although we do know a few things about him ...

We know he wears strange clothes which belong to earlier times, so he is probably quite old. He has charms and lures, all sewn or pinned or tied to his coat. In his pockets he keeps sweets and sours, and pieces of paper with messages on them.

Over his shoulder he carries a long bamboo pole with strange markings, which he uses to carry cages and traps he needs for collecting the dream creatures he finds. Sometimes he plays the bamboo pole as a flute. On his head he always wears an old stovepipe hat.

Many people believe that it's The Dreamkeeper
who catches our bad dreams when they try to
escape to become real. He is the one who knows the
tricks needed to lure, catch and return the
bad dream creatures to the safety of The Great
Dreamtree.

The Dreamkeeper designs and weaves all his
own cages and baskets, and each one is able to carry
a particular creature like a witch, a troll or a goblin –
or even a very small dragon.

Dragons are difficult to catch. They are larger than almost any creature you can dream about, and more dangerous.

When he catches dragons, The Dreamkeeper quickly shrinks them with a mild reducing potion made from the juice of houseflies.

Once this is done they can be carried in a sling, since they are often still too large for baskets.

Witches are also quite hard to catch. With the help of an ancient recipe, The Dreamkeeper prepares a powerful cocktail of bad-smelling herbs to make his job easier.

With each full moon some witches try to sneak away from the coven to make mischief in reality. To stop them, The Dreamkeeper sets up an elderwood tripod on the route usually taken by loose witches. A dish is balanced on the tripod, and the herb mixture is lit and allowed to burn. The fumes will turn any witch into a raven for a short time. And ravens are easy to catch.

The recipe for the witch herb brew was invented
by The Dreamkeeper's sister. She lives and works
far away in an old pigeonhouse on stilts somewhere in the south of France. She works in her
kitchen laboratory to keep her brother supplied
with dream-catching aids, like magic sweets
and sours, and of course her famous potion of
Belief Syrup.

For centuries pigeons have lived in pigeonhouses, and they still do. People think they are kept there to be hunted, or to make droppings in order to fertilize the surrounding vineyards. But they really carry messages for The College of Great Belief which has its offices in this building. The president of the College is The Dreamkeeper, and when he is not traveling he lives there with his sister and a useful goblin called Tally.

There are many pigeonhouses in rural France, particularly in the south, and nobody knows exactly which is the one where the College operates. Perhaps the offices move from one to another so that we humans remain confused.

The College of Great Belief operates for the well-being of storybook characters, and sometimes for real people who appear in stories.

Although we do not know who is on the Council of the College, we do know that Tally is the Council Secretary. He runs the day-to-day affairs of the College when he is not out dream-catching with his master.

Inside the pigeonhouse Tally has a small room with a bed for sleeping, a box for keeping, and a desk for recording and reporting.

The room has two doors: one that leads to the kitchen where Belief Syrup and other magic potions are made, and another that leads to the library and meeting chamber where The Dreamkeeper bunks down when he needs to sleep. A small window high in the room leads to the wider world outside.

Until recently people believed
that The Dreamkeeper worked
alone and had no helpers.

   This is not so; Tally is with
him at all times unless he is contracted
to do special projects for other council members.
He keeps a tally of all The Dreamkeeper's tricks,
captures and conquests.

   He has a memory as long as his white beard,
which he has to tuck into his belt to stop
tripping over himself. Once he used to
carry a sword to cut up his food and
defend himself, but now he makes do with
his ingenious belief-powered remote control.

Goblins, elves, imps, gnomes and trolls are members of a family generally devoted to interrupting peaceful dreams.

They regularly escape the safety of The Great Dreamtree to upset the peace and quiet of humans. For example, they can make themselves invisible to most boys and girls, and certainly to all grown-ups.

The Dreamkeeper uses Tally, a tamed goblin, to make sure you will only imagine that you can see them. With his specially designed remote control Tally can expose the presence of any tricky goblin or hairy troll. Once they are no longer invisible it is easy for The Dreamkeeper to lure them into his baskets with colorful licorice devised by his clever sister.

Under the protection of the many branches of The Great Dreamtree, good and evil spirits dwell in harmony with the creatures of dreams.

The Dreamkeeper knows that spirits, like ghosts, have a shape but no body, and that only bad spirits cast shadows. The scary shadows you see on the wall or ceiling at night often mark the presence of an escaped bad spirit up to no good. The Dreamkeeper has memorized the right words and songs to persuade these spirits to behave themselves and return.

When he speaks his voice is as soft as moss, and his words as gentle as a falling feather. He plays beautiful music on his long bamboo flute to lure and seduce runaway spirits back to the fabulous Great Dreamtree...

Now, Alice, I expect you have been waiting to hear how The Dreamkeeper catches and carries The Fairies. Well, I have a surprise for you; he doesn't. He couldn't even if he wanted to, because The Fairies, like shadows, cannot be caught. They are free to come and go whenever, however and wherever they like, forever.

You see, The Fairies do not live within
the branches and roots of the Great Dreamtree.
They dwell inside hollow hills or great mounds
of earth built by prehistoric tribes, either as
forts or monuments to past heroes. Humans
are advised to avoid these places, especially
after dark. However, like most dream creatures,
The Fairies must come to the Great Dreamtree
to die. That is probably why you never find
fairy rings in the garden.

So now you know about The Dreamkeeper.
He will never be far away when your mind is
somewhere between what is really happening
and what you imagine might happen.
     He lives in a world just around the corner
of your mind, where reality is an intruder and
dreams, both good and bad, come true.
And that's where you may find him and Tally.
     Safe traveling, good dreaming,
and God bless,

     Grandpa